Snapshot Timmy

EGMONT

First Published in Great Britain in 2010
by Egmont UK Limited
239 Kensington High Street, London W8 6SA

Series created and produced by Jackie Cockle
Based on a script by Dave Ingham

Printed in China

The clouds had started to clear
and the sun was shining over
the Nursery courtyard.

Osbourne popped his head out the door.
He looked at the puddles on the ground
and then at the clear sky above. Holding his
wing out he checked for any raindrops.

Osbourne nodded in satisfaction.
Perfect weather for the Nursery
photograph he thought!

Meanwhile in the Nursery cloakroom,
the little animals were very excited about
getting their photograph taken.
They could not wait to smile at the camera!

Everybody peered at Osbourne as he
gathered together his equipment.
With Otus' help, he took it outside
into the Nursery courtyard.

The little animals followed,
as Harriet ushered them outside.

Harriet fussed and flapped, making sure all the little animals were looking their best.

Meanwhile, Timmy noticed the puddles. He giggled in excitement.

BAAH! BAAH!

Timmy jumped into the middle of a puddle!

BAAH! BAAH!

He was having a great time as he danced around and splashed in the muddy puddle!

As the little animals lined up for the photograph, Yabba noticed Timmy having fun and wanted to join her friend.

Timmy and Yabba splashed around in the muddy puddle.

QUACK! QUACK!

Yabba was delighted!

The two little friends played together in the puddle – they were covered in mud but they didn't care, splashing was so much fun!

Meanwhile, Osbourne and Otus were busy setting up the camera.

HOOT! HOOT!

Osbourne positioned the camera on the tripod and handed the duster to Otus who polished the camera lens.

Osbourne nodded with approval at Otus and then glanced at the sky to check the light.

Finally, the little animals were ready! Osbourne framed the scene with his wings, but where were Timmy and Yabba?

Everyone turned to see Timmy and Yabba.
They were covered in mud!

Osbourne shook his head, whilst Harriet led the
muddy duo inside to clean them up.

QUACK! QUACK!

Harriet scrubbed the mud off Yabba.

BAAH! BAAH!

Timmy waited his turn.

At last, the two little animals were sparkling
clean. Harriet dried them off and led them back
to their places in the front row.

Everybody was in position and beaming at the camera lens. Osbourne set the timer on the camera and quickly rushed to join them.

Tick . . . **tick** . . . **tick** . . . went the timer.

Suddenly, the cuckoo popped out of the clock tower – it was playtime!

CLICK! Went the camera, just as the little animals rushed to the playground, leaving Osbourne, Harriet and Otus smiling at the camera. Osbourne sighed, not one of the little animals were in the photograph!

In the playground, the little animals were having fun. Timmy spotted Paxton playing football.

BAAH! BAAH!

Timmy **LOVED** football.

Paxton kicked the ball to Timmy, who charged at the ball and flicked it high into the air with his little hoof!

All the little animals stopped what they were doing and watched as the ball flew high up into the sky and landed right in the middle of a rather large, muddy puddle!

One by one, Harriet scrubbed all the little animals clean. Once again, Osbourne called everyone back into the courtyard for the photo.

The little animals were ready and took their places. Osbourne pressed the button on the timer, waddling back to take his place. Suddenly there was a **PLOP!** It had started to rain!

CLICK went the camera just as everyone rushed indoors, followed quickly by Osbourne carrying the camera and Otus wearing a sou'wester hat!

Osbourne was setting the camera up
in the classroom when the cuckoo
popped out of the clock. Lunch time!
Everyone rushed to get their lunch boxes
and quietly sat down to eat their lunch.

Timmy peered into his lunch box.
Jam sandwiches - his favourite!

Mittens sat beside Timmy, as he took an
extra-large bite of his sandwich - the jam squirted
all over her! Oh no, Timmy was
very sorry and watched as Harriet
cleaned Mittens' face with a cloth.

Osbourne gathered the little animals around and
again they took their places for the photo.
Everyone was finally ready and smiling
at the camera.

Osbourne pressed the timer button and
hurried to take his place with the others.

Everyone smiled, and waited for the camera.
They waited . . . and waited . . . and waited.

But the camera did not click.

Osbourne checked the camera to see what was wrong with it. He peered into the lens and tapped the top of the camera.

Suddenly, there was a **CLUNK**, then there was a **SNAP**, followed shortly by a loud **CLICK!**

Poor, Osbourne! The camera worked just as he was peering into the lens, taking a blurred close up of his face!

Osbourne looked a bit dazed, he blinked and scratched his head. He had an idea. If he put the button on a longer cable, he could stand in his place and then press the button!

Osbourne searched in the camera case for a longer cable. **HOOT HOOT!** He'd found one!

Attaching the cable to the camera, he made his way back to the class. This time, Osbourne was going to get it right, he was ready to press the button.

As the little animals shuffled around, Osbourne took his place.

HOOT! HOOT! He called out.

Harriet hushed everyone and they all looked straight ahead and smiled widely!

ONE, TWO, THREE! Osbourne pushed the button, but nothing happened. He shook the cable and pressed the button again . . .

But the cable had caught on the bookshelves behind. **PLOP!** A tin of red paint flew up into the air and landed with a splat on Osbourne's head!

Osbourne stood still, the red paint running down his face, still clutching the cable in one wing! He dropped the cable in surprise and quick-thinking Otus caught it.

Suddenly, there was a **CLICK!** Otus had saved the day and pressed the button. Finally, the photo had been taken! The little animals cheered!

The class photo was wonderful! This time everyone was smiling - even Osbourne was grinning through the bright red paint!